The Enormous Turnip

illustrated by
Barbara Bailey

Once upon a time there was an old man
who had a vegetable patch in his garden.
He grew cabbages, lettuces and beans.
One year he decided to grow some turnips.
So he sowed a few rows of turnip seeds.
As the weeks went by the earth was warmed
by the sun and wetted by the rain.
The turnips began to grow.
They sent up little green shoots.

Every day the old man went to see his turnips.
They all grew a bit bigger but one turnip
was growing much faster than the others.
It was getting larger and larger.
It grew up to his ankles, then up to his knees,
then almost up to his waist!
No one had ever seen such an enormous turnip.

One day the old man decided it was time
to pull up the turnip.
He changed into his gardening trousers,
put on his boots and went out to the garden.
With both hands he took hold of the large
green leaves and gave them a tug.
The turnip didn't move an inch.
He took a deep breath and pulled harder,
but still the turnip would not move.
He pulled and pulled and went red in the face
but he could not pull up the enormous turnip.

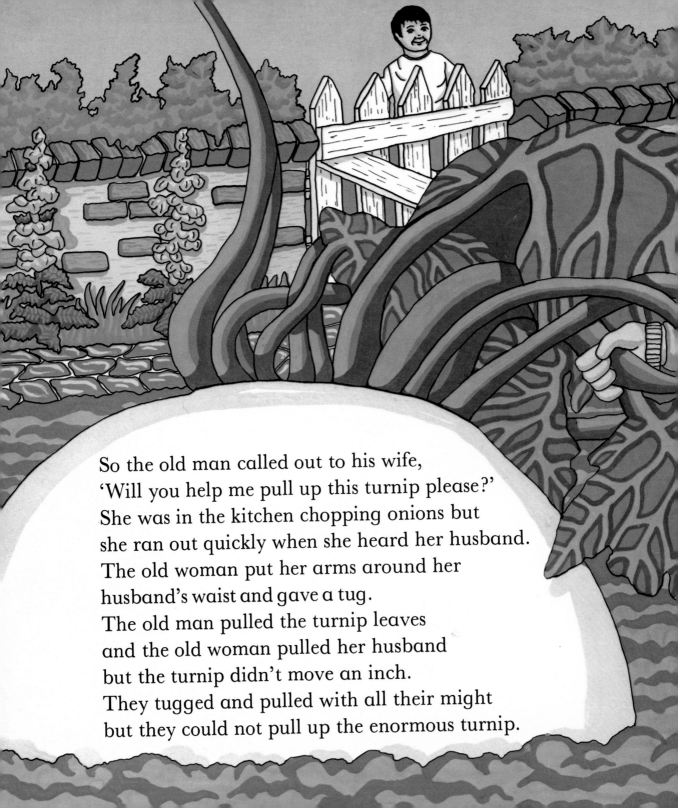

So the old man called out to his wife,
'Will you help me pull up this turnip please?'
She was in the kitchen chopping onions but
she ran out quickly when she heard her husband.
The old woman put her arms around her
husband's waist and gave a tug.
The old man pulled the turnip leaves
and the old woman pulled her husband
but the turnip didn't move an inch.
They tugged and pulled with all their might
but they could not pull up the enormous turnip.

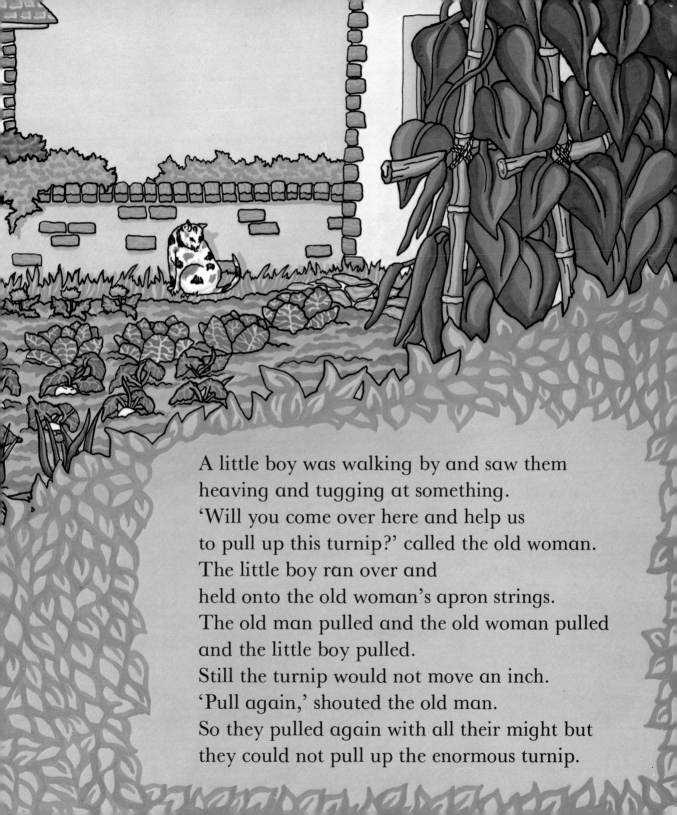

A little boy was walking by and saw them
heaving and tugging at something.
'Will you come over here and help us
to pull up this turnip?' called the old woman.
The little boy ran over and
held onto the old woman's apron strings.
The old man pulled and the old woman pulled
and the little boy pulled.
Still the turnip would not move an inch.
'Pull again,' shouted the old man.
So they pulled again with all their might but
they could not pull up the enormous turnip.

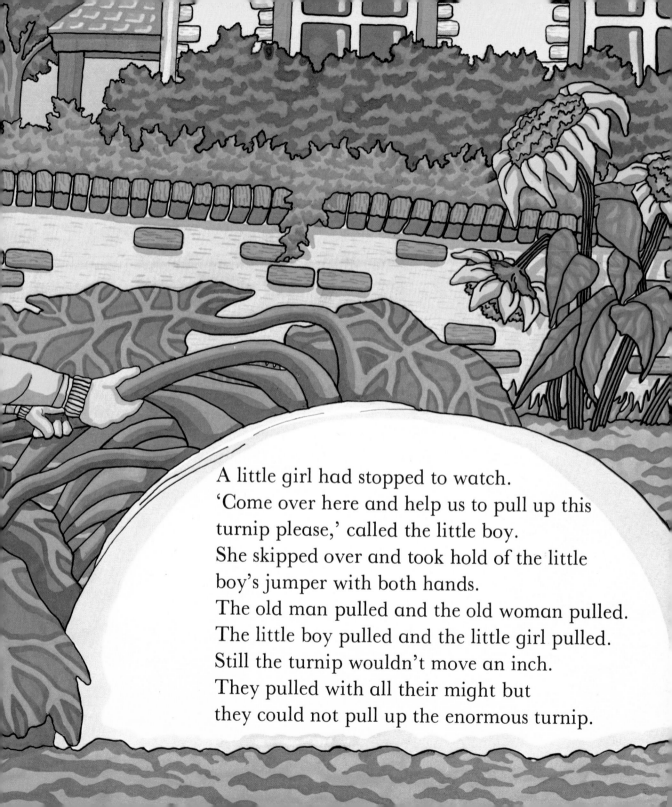

A little girl had stopped to watch.
'Come over here and help us to pull up this
turnip please,' called the little boy.
She skipped over and took hold of the little
boy's jumper with both hands.
The old man pulled and the old woman pulled.
The little boy pulled and the little girl pulled.
Still the turnip wouldn't move an inch.
They pulled with all their might but
they could not pull up the enormous turnip.

So the little girl called to a big dog,
'Come here and help us to pull up this turnip.'
The big dog bounded over and held onto the
hem of the little girl's dress with his teeth.
Then the old man pulled and the old woman pulled.
The little boy pulled and the little girl pulled
and the big dog pulled.
Still the turnip would not move an inch.
They pulled again with all their might but
they could not pull up the enormous turnip.

A cat was lazing in the sun.
'Come here and help us to pull up this turnip please,' barked the dog to the cat.
The cat took hold of the big dog's tail.
Then the old man and the old woman pulled.
The little boy and the little girl pulled.
The big dog pulled and the cat pulled.
Still the turnip would not move an inch.
Everyone was getting very tired and they just could not pull up the enormous turnip.

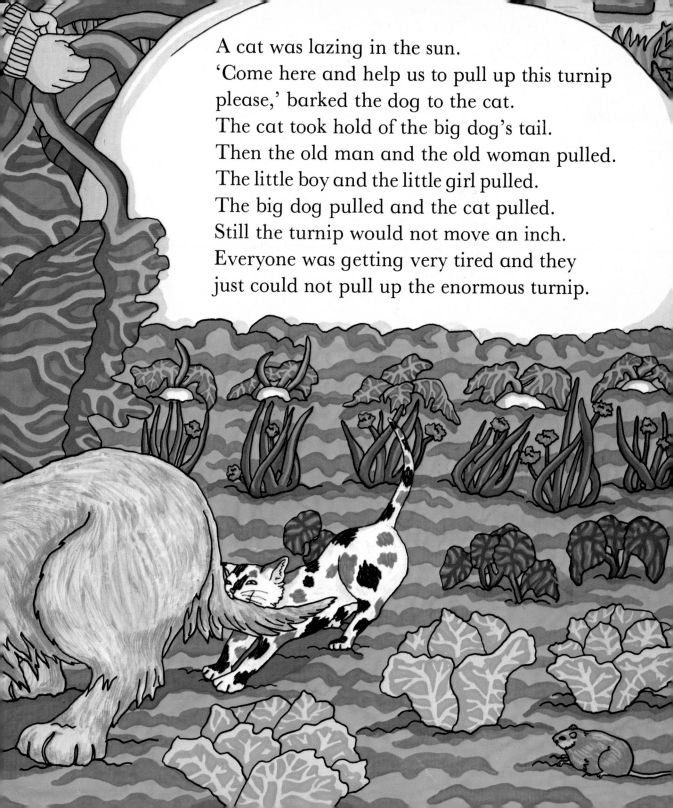

All this time a little mouse was watching them.
The cat spied him and called,
'Will you help us pull up this turnip?'
The little mouse scampered over and
took hold of the end of the cat's tail.
He gave a tiny tug and . . . .

. . . the enormous turnip flew out of the ground!
Everybody toppled over.
The turnip fell on top of the old man.
The old man fell on top of the old woman.
The old woman fell on top of the little boy.
The little boy fell on the little girl.
The little girl fell on the big dog.
The big dog fell on the cat and
the cat nearly squashed the tiny mouse!
But nobody was hurt and they all jumped up,
brushed themselves down and started to laugh.